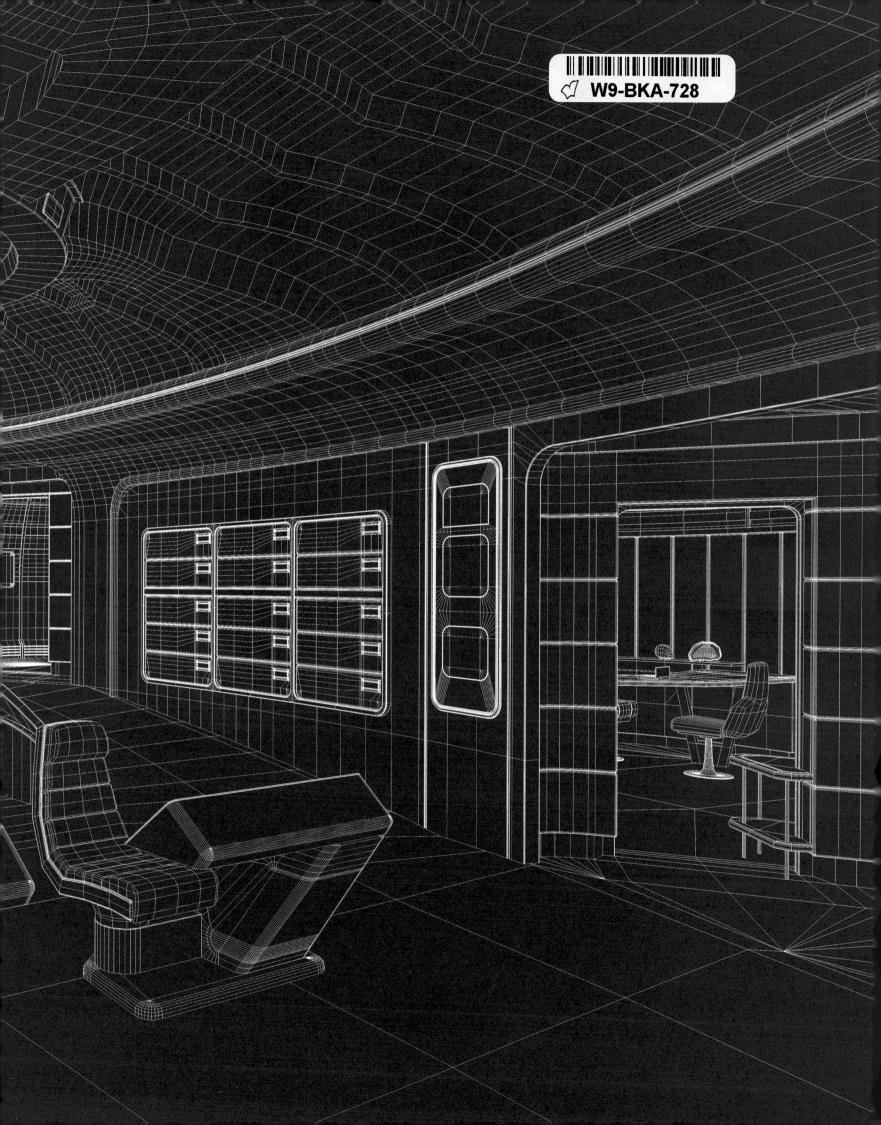

STAR TREK™

THE NEXT GENERATION

First edition for North America published in 2013
by Barron's Educational Series, Inc.

All inquiries should be addressed to:
Barron's Educational Series, Inc.
250 Wireless Boulevard
Hauppauge, NY 11788
www.barronseduc.com

Published in Great Britain in 2013 by Carlton Books Limited,
An imprint of the Carlton Publishing Group
20 Mortimer Street
London W1T 3JW

ISBN: 978-0-7641-6606-8

Library of Congress Control No.: 2012951855

Graphic Artists: Somchith Vongprachanh and Tobias Richter.

Printed in China
9 8 7 6 5 4 3 2 1

STAR TREK™
THE NEXT GENERATION

ON BOARD THE U.S.S. ENTERPRISE®

BE TRANSPORTED TO THE FINAL FRONTIER WITH A BREATHTAKING 3D TOUR

BY DENISE AND MICHAEL OKUDA

BARRON'S

CONTENTS

27 031976

001 0818210
296 9910296
871 1728191
       8818210
340 5325406
6   3096700

40271

INTRODUCTION:
Denise and Michael Okuda

WE SPENT SEVERAL YEARS OF OUR LIVES ON THE *STARSHIP ENTERPRISE*. REALLY.

We speak, of course, about being part of the *Star Trek* production family at Paramount. Mike was lead graphic designer on *Star Trek: The Next Generation* and the other spinoffs, plus several of the movies. Denise served occasionally as a medical consultant, in addition to her duties as video supervisor and scenic artist. We also worked with our friend David Rossi as producers on CBS's remastered version of the original *Star Trek* series.

Maybe it wasn't quite as exciting as being a crew member on a Federation starship – going boldly where none have gone before – but trust us, it was a whole lot of fun.

We were proud to be part of a great team, working together on a challenging mission. Creating a futuristic starship and its fantastic destinations every week meant a lot of long, exhausting hours for all of us. That's how the *U.S.S. Enterprise* became a home to us, and why our friends on the production crew became our extended family.

Of course, we never lost sight of what brought us to *Star Trek* to begin with. We're both lifelong fans of science fiction and supporters of the real-life space program. To us, *Star Trek* personifies both. And standing on those beautiful sets was like bringing them both to life.

That was 25 years ago. Production on *Star Trek: The Next Generation* has long since ended. The sets have been dismantled, and the surviving props and models have mostly disappeared into collections around the world. That's fine with us (although we'd be lying if we didn't say we wished we had one or two of those models in our living room.) We always knew that all those cool toys were simply tools to create images on film. Those images – and the dreams and stories that they represent – are what really count.

Now, amazingly enough, it seems that we're once again living on the *U.S.S. Enterprise*. Turns out that a lot of people remember and love *Star Trek: The Next Generation*.

We have been working with CBS on remastering episodes in high definition. It is fascinating work, and it's given us the pleasure of revisiting that lovely spaceship, now even more beautiful than ever in glorious high definition. Frankly, we'd forgotten how much we loved that ship and those sets. We were so incredibly lucky to work with such great talents as production designers Herman Zimmerman and Richard James. Not to mention brilliant illustrators Andrew Probert and Rick Sternbach, set decorators John Dwyer and Jimmy Mees, plus the talented art directors, set designers, scenic artists, model makers, and all of our other colleagues. Good people, all.

That's why we're so excited about this book. It has given us a chance to further rediscover the good ship *U.S.S. Enterprise*. Even better, the computer artistry of the amazing Tobias Richter and Somchith Vongprachanh has been used to create detailed new renderings of those sets, as well as of the *Enterprise*-D, herself.

We hope you'll join us in taking this virtual tour of one of our favorite starships. We hope you'll pause here and there to recall the great adventures of Captain Picard and company. And we hope you'll share, once again, the sense of family of being on board the flagship of the Federation, voyaging into the final frontier.

And it's that sense of family that binds us all together – fans, friends, and filmmakers alike – in that wondrous world that is Gene Roddenberry's vision of the future. Whether you're a long-time fan or someone who's lucky enough to have just discovered the voyages of the *U.S.S. Enterprise*, welcome.

Let's see what's out there, together.

Michael and Denise Okuda
Los Angeles, CA
Sector 001

STARFLEET:
History of the *Enterprise*

The space frontier continues to challenge our civilization as it offers ever-expanding opportunities for growth and discovery. Indeed, the exploration of space is the great adventure that defines the culture of the Federation.

Leading this great enterprise is Starfleet, the Federation's deep-space exploratory corps whose mission is to explore strange new worlds, to seek out new life and new civilizations, and to boldly go where no one has gone before.

Even after nearly three centuries of interstellar exploration, only 19 percent of our Galaxy has been mapped. This is the mission of the Federation Starfleet, including the *Galaxy*-class *Starship Enterprise*-D. The *Enterprise* and her sister ships of Starfleet are amazing vehicles, but there remains so many places to explore, so much to see, and unimagined wonders to discover.

The predecessors of the *Enterprise*-D have been among the best-known craft in space exploration. The first *Starship Enterprise* was one of the first ships to explore large distances using warp drive. Under the command of Captain Jonathan Archer, this ship saved Earth during the Xindi War, and later played a role in the founding of the Federation.

The first Federation starship to bear the name *Enterprise* (NCC-1701) blazed a trail into the unknown and became one of the most famous space vehicles in history. The *Enterprise*-C became known for the courage of her captain and crew in intervening in a deadly battle between the Klingons and the Romulans.

Long before the birth of the Federation, ships named *Enterprise* have been the stuff of legend.

The first ship of the 18th century American navy was a sloop-of-war called *Enterprise*. Another ship with the same name was Earth's first nuclear-powered aircraft carrier, a massive ocean-going vessel that participated in the recovery of one of the first Earth orbital spaceflights. Yet another *Enterprise* was the prototype for Earth's first reusable orbital space vehicle.

One of Earth's first interstellar spacecraft was the *Enterprise* XCV-330, a pre-Starfleet vessel that employed an unusual annular warp propulsion system, based on technology borrowed from the Vulcans.

Among the distinguished men and women who have commanded spaceships named *Enterprise* are many famous explorers, scientists, and diplomats.

The first commander of a spaceship named *Enterprise* was astronaut Fred Haise, who gained fame as a crew member on an early lunar expedition called *Apollo 13*, which nearly ended in disaster. Haise's *Enterprise* was the space shuttle *Enterprise* OV-101.

Captain Jonathan Archer, commander of the *Enterprise* NX-01, was responsible for saving Earth from annihilation during the Xindi war, and later served as president of the United Federation of Planets.

ABOVE: THE FIRST *U.S.S. ENTERPRISE*, WHICH WAS SO NAMED IN 1775. IT STARTED LIFE AS A QUEBEC, CANADA-MADE SLOOP THAT THE BRITISH CALLED *GEORGE*.

ABOVE: FRED W. HAISE JR. WAS COMMANDER OF THE SPACE SHUTTLE *ENTERPRISE* IN 1977. HE WAS PART OF THE THIRD MISSION INTENDED TO LAND ON EARTH'S MOON.

Captain James T. Kirk commanded the *Enterprise* NCC-1701 on numerous missions of exploration, diplomacy, and defense.

Captain Rachel Garrett led the *Starship Enterprise*-C and her crew into the deadly battle of Narendra III. Their heroic sacrifice is credited with preventing a war between the Federation and the Klingon Empire.

Like many of her predecessors, the *Galaxy*-class *Starship Enterprise*-D is too big to build on a planetary surface. Although her components were built at the Utopia Planitia Fleet Yards on Mars, final assembly was accomplished in martian orbit at a drydock facility.

ABOVE: THE FOURTH INCARNATION OF THE CURRENT ERA *U.S.S. ENTERPRISE*, THE NCC-1701-D. IT WAS COMMISSIONED ON OCTOBER 4, 2363, THE 406TH ANNIVERSARY OF MANKIND'S FIRST SPACE LAUNCH.

LEFT: THE *U.S.S. ENTERPRISE* (CVN-65) WAS THE WORLD'S FIRST NUCLEAR-POWERED AIRCRAFT CARRIER, COMMISSIONED ON NOVEMBER 25, 1961. NICKNAMED THE 'BIG E', SHE WAS THE LONGEST NAVAL VESSEL OF HER ERA.

001	0019210
296	9910296
671	1728191
	8819210
340	5325406
6	3096700
640	5604100
712	9012
781	8563909

ABOVE: THE *ENTERPRISE* OV-101 WAS THE VERY FIRST SPACE SHUTTLE ORBITER. ALTHOUGH SHE NEVER MADE IT TO SPACE, SHE WAS COMPLETED ON SEPTEMBER 17, 1976 AND FLEW SEVERAL TEST VOYAGES DURING 1977.

ABOVE: LAUNCHED IN 2123, THE *U.S.S. ENTERPRISE* (XCV 330) WAS HUMANITY'S FIRST INTERSTELLAR LINER, AND THE FIRST TRUE STARSHIP TO BEAR THE FAMOUS NAME. ALMOST 1000FT LONG, IT HELD 850 PASSENGERS AND 100 CREW.

TO BOLDLY GO:
Memorable voyages of discovery

001 0019210
296 9910296
671 1728191
   8819210
340 5325406
8   3096700
840 5804100
712 9012
781 8563909

451 06

The distances to the stars are so incredibly great that the only way to reach them is with a warp-powered starship. Even though long-range sensing and astronomical telescopes make it possible to study stars and planets from great distances, the only way to truly know them is to visit them.

The Milky Way Galaxy is about 100,000 light years in diameter and contains some 100 billion stars. Many of those stars are hosts to planets. Some of those planets are home to unknown life-forms. Others hold wonders and resources yet undiscovered.

The voyage of the *Starship Enterprise*-D is but the latest chapter in Starfleet's proud mission to find out what is out there on those unknown planets in star systems, many of which have not yet even been discovered.

One of the first missions of the *Enterprise*-D was to investigate a new starbase facility that had been built on planet Deneb IV. Although the facility appeared to be nearly ideal for Starfleet's needs, investigation by *Enterprise* personnel uncovered the surprising fact that the "starbase" was, indeed, a previously-unknown spaceborne life-form with the ability to change shape. Thanks to the intervention of the *Enterprise* and her crew, this life-form was able to return to space, where it rejoined its mate.

Another remarkable new life-form was a cloud entity accidentally discovered by the *Enterprise*-D crew near the Beta Renner star system. This intelligent entity was actually capable of moving at warp speeds. It was captured by the *Enterprise*, where it found the ship's crew, especially Captain Picard, to be a kindred spirit. Nevertheless, the entity's joining with Picard would have destroyed Picard's consciousness had the *Enterprise* crew not been successful in separating the two.

The *Enterprise*-D and her crew inadvertently became major players in Klingon politics when the father of Tactical Officer Worf was falsely accused of treason against the Klingon Empire. Captain Picard ordered the *Enterprise* to transport Worf to the Klingon homeworld so that he could personally assist with Worf's defense.

ABOVE: THE *ENTERPRISE*-D IN ORBIT ABOVE A MINSHARA-CLASS PLANET. SUITABLE FOR HUMANOID LIFE, M-CLASS PLANETS ARE HIGHLY SOUGHT. A PRIME EXAMPLE IS ARCHER IV IN THE 61 URSAE MAJORIS SYSTEM.

The first known Federation contact with the Ferengi occurred in 2364 when the Enterprise-D intercepted a Ferengi marauder ship that was believed to be carrying a valuable piece of Federation technology. During the course of the mission, both the Enterprise and the Ferengi ship made first contact with a representative of the T'Kon Empire, an ancient civilization long believed extinct. Perhaps the deadliest adversary facing the Federation in the past century is the Borg Collective. In 2365, the Enterprise-D became the first Starfleet ship to make contact with the Borg. A year later, the Enterprise was on the front lines of defense when a Borg ship penetrated Federation space and reached Sector 001 and Earth orbit. During the incursion, Enterprise captain Picard was kidnapped by the Borg and assimilated into the Collective. Fortunately, Enterprise personnel were able to recover Picard and were successful in extracting him from Borg control.

The ancient Iconians were once believed to be mere myth, known as "demons of air and darkness" in ancient texts. Captain Picard and the Enterprise crew, following up on research by Captain Donald Varley of the Starship Yamato, actually discovered the Iconian home planet, deep in the Romulan Neutral Zone. Although the Iconians and the surface of their planet had long been devastated in an ancient battle, fragments of their civilization survived. Picard and his team discovered ancient "gateway" technology that allowed the Iconians to traverse the Galaxy without the use of ships.

Even traveling above Warp 9, the Enterprise and other starships are essentially limited to exploration within our own Milky Way because of the stupendous distances to other galaxies. Even the nearby Andromeda Galaxy is some 1,200 years away at maximum cruising speed. Nevertheless, an unusual individual called The Traveler made it possible for the Enterprise to visit Galaxy M33, also known as Triangulum. Although their visit was brief, members of the Enterprise crew were treated to the extraordinary vista of that distant galaxy, truly where no one had gone before.

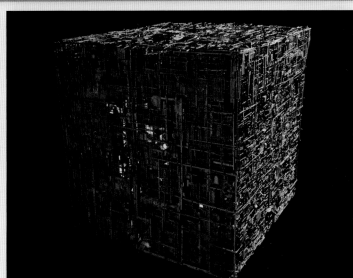

LEFT: A FERENGI, FROM THE HOME PLANET FERENGINAR.

TOP: 2364, AND THE ENTERPRISE-D BIDS FAREWELL TO THE SPACEBORNE ENTITY THAT THEY RESCUED FROM ENSLAVEMENT BY THE BANDI PEOPLE ON DENEB IV.

ABOVE RIGHT: THE KLINGON HOMEWORLD OF QO'NOS WAS FIRST VISITED BY HUMANITY IN 2151. IN THIS PICTURE, TAKEN IN 2366, WE SEE THE HISTORIC OLD QUARTER OF THE FIRST CITY, NEAR THE GREAT HALL.

RIGHT: A DARING SHOT OF A BORG CUBE. THE TRAGIC MASSACRE OF 40 STARFLEET SHIPS BY A SINGLE CUBE IN ONE BATTLE IS A CHILLING TESTAMENT TO THE POWER OF THE COLLECTIVE.

U.S.S. ENTERPRISE EXTERIOR DORSAL

WARP DRIVE NACELLES
These generate the all-important subspace field that warps space and makes it possible for the Enterprise to travel faster than the speed of light.

MAIN PYLON
Connecting the Saucer Module to the Engineering Hull, this is the ship's structural backbone. Located at the top is the Battle Bridge, and the docking clamps that hold the ship together during normal flight.

BUSSARD COLLECTORS
Located at the front of each warp nacelle. They use electromagnetic fields to collect free hydrogen molecules found in interstellar space.

MAIN SHUTTLEBAY
The Main Shuttlebay is the primary base of operations for launch, recovery, and servicing of shuttlecraft.

SAUCER IMPULSE ENGINE

AFT PHOTON TORPEDO LAUNCHER
Provides additional tactical coverage, especially for pursuing adversaries.

MAIN IMPULSE ENGINE
The Main Impulse Engine operates at slower-than-light speeds, and thus is rarely used during interstellar travel. Nevertheless, impulse propulsion is often employed for travel between planets of a single solar system.

STARDRIVE SECTION
The ship's engineering hull, plus the warp nacelles and the main pylon comprise the Stardrive Section, also known as the Battle Section. This section also contains sufficient crew quarters and support facilities for operation when the ship section is separated from the Saucer Module.

ENGINEERING HULL
The largest single component of the Stardrive Section is the Engineering Hull, which houses the ship's main matter/antimatter reactor, the power source of the ship's warp drive system. The Engineering Hull also houses the powerful main deflector and the long-range sensor systems.

SHUTTLEBAY 2 AND SHUTTLEBAY 3
Located on the aft of the main pylon, are Shuttlebays 2 and 3 smaller facilities for shuttlecraft launch, recovery, and maintenance. In addition to serving as backups to the Main Shuttlebay, these two facilities support operations of the Enterprise stardrive section when in separated from the Saucer Module.

U.S.S. ENTERPRISE

A Galaxy-class explorer, the *U.S.S. Enterprise* (NCC-1701-D) is the flagship of the Federation. She was built at the Utopia Planitia Fleet Yards in orbit around Mars under the close supervision of Commander Orfil Quinteros, and commissioned on October 4, 2363. After a final check-over at McKinley Station, Rear Admiral Satie ordered command of the ship to go to Captain Jean-Luc Picard. Captain Picard assumed his post on February 23, 2364.

947

88

BUSSARD COLLECTOR

SAUCER IMPULSE ENGINES
The Saucer Impulse Engines provide backup propulsion to the Saucer Module when it is separated from the Stardrive Section.

WARP ENGINE NACELLE

REACTION CONTROL THRUSTER

WARP ENGINE FIELD GRILL

NCC-1701·D

ENTERPRISE

RIGHT: THE STARBOARD VIEW OF THE *ENTERPRISE*-D. NOTE THE HIGHLY DETAILED DECK SCHEMATICS.

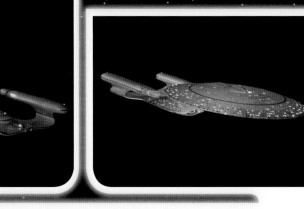

20
368
72
008

407

686
102
23

PHASER BANK

AFT PHOTON TORPEDO LAUNCHER

ABOVE: PERSPECTIVE VIEWS OF THE *STARSHIP ENTERPRISE* IN FLIGHT.

SAUCER MODULE

Also called the Primary Hull, the main section of the *Enterprise* houses most of the crew and most mission-critical facilities. In an emergency, the Saucer Module can separate from the ship's Stardrive Section, also known as the Battle Section. The Saucer Module is incapable of warp flight without the Stardrive Section.

OBSERVATION LOUNGE

The Conference room, directly behind the main bridge, offers a quiet place for the captain to convene senior staff and is isolated from the operational activity of the main bridge. The Observation Lounge features large windows, offering a spectacular vista.

MAIN BRIDGE

Located on Deck 1, the Main Bridge is the command center from which the entire ship's operation is controlled. Not only are helm, navigation, and tactical functions managed from the bridge, but also engineering and propulsion.

UMBILICAL CONNECT POINTS

Although transporters and shuttles are the most commonly used methods for resupply, the *Enterprise* is equipped with a number of umbilical connect points that allow it to be powered and resupplied from an external source.

PHASER BANK

The ship's primary tactical weapons system, these generate and direct coherent energy with great precision toward a target. The *Enterprise* has a number of phaser banks, located at various positions around the hull.

CAPTAIN'S READY ROOM

A small office adjacent to the bridge, providing the captain with a private workspace, while allowing him or her to remain close to the ship's command center.

TRANSPORTER EMITTER

These are the actual antennas for the ship's transporter beams. They use phased arrays which can direct a beam with great precision in nearly any direction.

ESCAPE POD

As a last resort in an emergency, the ship's crew can evacuate the ship using escape pods.

LIVING QUARTERS

The ship carries 1012 crew and attached personnel. Living quarters are designed for both efficiency and comfort, two qualities that are of great importance on extended missions into the unknown. Some of the quarters in the saucer module feature large windows, providing a dramatic view of the cosmos.

U.S.S. ENTERPRISE EXTERIOR VENTRAL

WARP NACELLE

BUSSARD COLLECTOR

MAIN DEFLECTOR

SAUCER IMPULSE ENGINE

Two fusion-powered impulse propulsion units provide Newtonian thrust for slower-than-light travel. In addition to serving as a backup to the ship's main impulse engine, the Saucer Impulse Engines provide propulsion to the Saucer Module when separated from the Stardrive Section.

TRACTOR BEAM EMITTER

The tractor beam is used to tow small objects or to hold them in close proximity of the ship. It uses a focused linear forcefield and can also serve as a mooring beam when the ship is docked.

NACELLE PYLON

The ship's graceful "wings" support the warp nacelles and hold them in the correct position, relative to the saucer module and engineering hull, to generate the optimal subspace field for warp flight.

WARP CORE EJECTION HATCH

In case of major malfunction with the warp drive system, the reactor core can be ejected to keep it from destroying the ship. In such an emergency, explosive bolts would blow open the ejection hatch, while force fields would attempt to contain the antimatter and the warp plasma until the warp reactor core can be pushed safely away from the ship. Naturally, this would only be attempted as a last resort, since the loss of the warp core would make the ship unable to travel at faster-than-light speeds.

CARGO LOADING DOOR

Opens directly into space, allowing direct transfer of large objects. In an emergency can also be used as an airlock or to support shuttle operations.

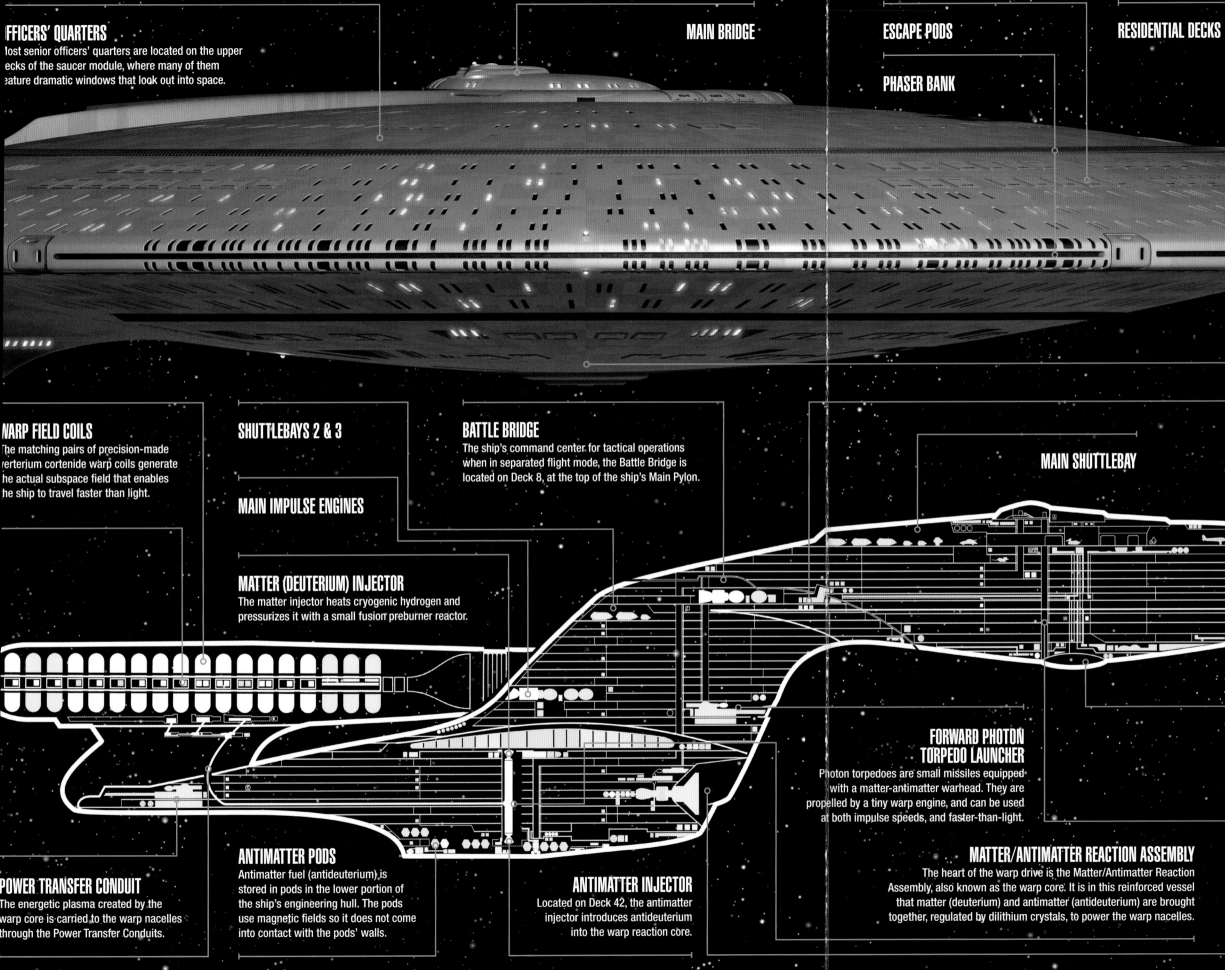

OFFICERS' QUARTERS
Most senior officers' quarters are located on the upper decks of the saucer module, where many of them feature dramatic windows that look out into space.

MAIN BRIDGE

ESCAPE PODS

PHASER BANK

RESIDENTIAL DECKS

TEN-FORWARD LOUNGE
Located on the forward rim of the saucer module, the Ten-Forward Lounge is the center of the crew's social life.

DOCKING PORT
Transporters and shuttles are the most common means of entering and leaving the ship, but the *Enterprise* is equipped with a number of docking ports, allowing direct connection to an external ship or facility.

WARP FIELD COILS
The matching pairs of precision-made verterium cortenide warp coils generate the actual subspace field that enables the ship to travel faster than light.

SHUTTLEBAYS 2 & 3

MAIN IMPULSE ENGINES

BATTLE BRIDGE
The ship's command center for tactical operations when in separated flight mode, the Battle Bridge is located on Deck 8, at the top of the ship's Main Pylon.

MAIN SHUTTLEBAY

DOCKING LATCHES
Located on the upper surface of the ship's Main Pylon, the docking latches literally hold the Saucer Module onto the Stardrive Section. Although these devices are extremely rigid and are designed to bear tremendous structural loads, they are reinforced by the energy of the ship's Structural Integrity Field, which helps the entire ship withstand the stresses of spaceflight.

MATTER (DEUTERIUM) INJECTOR
The matter injector heats cryogenic hydrogen and pressurizes it with a small fusion preburner reactor.

CAPTAIN'S YACHT
Also known as the Captain's Gig, this short-range vehicle is normally reserved for diplomatic missions and for the captain's personal use.

TURBOSHAFT
The ship's turbolift system provides high-speed access for the crew to nearly any part of the ship. Turbolifts are essential because of the ship's enormous size, and they greatly increase efficiency of crew operations.

FORWARD PHOTON TORPEDO LAUNCHER
Photon torpedoes are small missiles equipped with a matter-antimatter warhead. They are propelled by a tiny warp engine, and can be used at both impulse speeds, and faster-than-light.

POWER TRANSFER CONDUIT
The energetic plasma created by the warp core is carried to the warp nacelles through the Power Transfer Conduits.

ANTIMATTER PODS
Antimatter fuel (antideuterium) is stored in pods in the lower portion of the ship's engineering hull. The pods use magnetic fields so it does not come into contact with the pods' walls.

ANTIMATTER INJECTOR
Located on Deck 42, the antimatter injector introduces antideuterium into the warp reaction core.

MATTER/ANTIMATTER REACTION ASSEMBLY
The heart of the warp drive is the Matter/Antimatter Reaction Assembly, also known as the warp core. It is in this reinforced vessel that matter (deuterium) and antimatter (antideuterium) are brought together, regulated by dilithium crystals, to power the warp nacelles.

MAIN DEFLECTOR AND LONG RANGE SENSOR ARRAY
When the ship is traveling at warp speeds or even high impulse velocity, collision with even a tiny particle of dust could be catastrophic. That's why the ship's Main Deflector sweeps far ahead of the vessel, pushing aside meteoroids, debris, and even dust. The big deflector dish also houses the long-range sensor array, which helps to detect such hazards, and also serves many scientific and tactical functions.

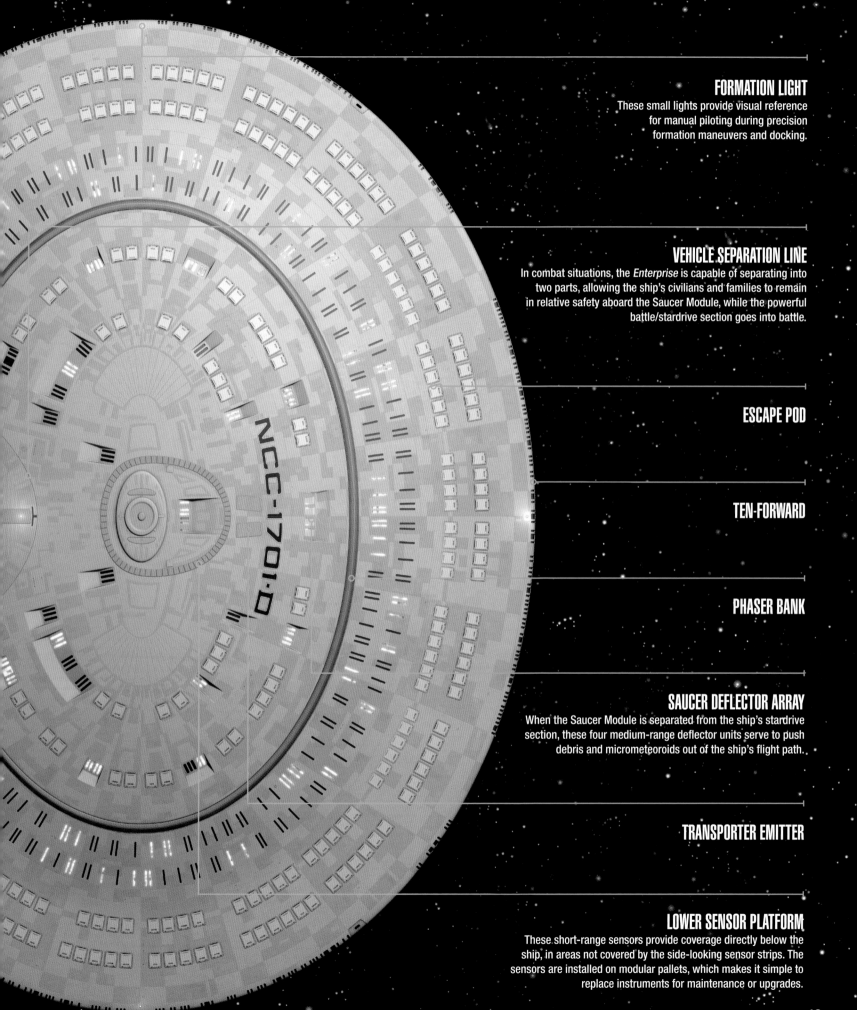

FORMATION LIGHT
These small lights provide visual reference for manual piloting during precision formation maneuvers and docking.

VEHICLE SEPARATION LINE
In combat situations, the *Enterprise* is capable of separating into two parts, allowing the ship's civilians and families to remain in relative safety aboard the Saucer Module, while the powerful battle/stardrive section goes into battle.

ESCAPE POD

TEN-FORWARD

PHASER BANK

SAUCER DEFLECTOR ARRAY
When the Saucer Module is separated from the ship's stardrive section, these four medium-range deflector units serve to push debris and micrometeoroids out of the ship's flight path.

TRANSPORTER EMITTER

LOWER SENSOR PLATFORM
These short-range sensors provide coverage directly below the ship, in areas not covered by the side-looking sensor strips. The sensors are installed on modular pallets, which makes it simple to replace instruments for maintenance or upgrades.

AFT STATIONS

Located on the back wall of the Main Bridge, the aft stations provide work stations for key personnel as needed.

SCIENCE I   **SCIENCE II**   **MISSION OPERATIONS**   **ENVIRONMENT**   **ENGINEERING**

READY ROOM

The ready room is a private office for the commanding officer, right next to the bridge. Captain Picard's ready room is decorated with a few personal items including a tropical fish tank, a painting of the *Starship Enterprise*, and an ancient book containing the collected works of Shakespeare.

COMMANDER WILLIAM T. RIKER

As the first officer and executive officer of the *Enterprise*, William T. Riker is directly responsible to the captain for keeping the ship and all personnel at peak operating efficiency. The first officer also has the responsibility to lead most Away Team missions, so that the captain is not placed at unnecessary risk. Riker is from Alaska, Earth. He enjoys poker and playing the trombone.

COUNSELOR DEANNA TROI

The ship's counselor provides the captain with guidance on the crew's emotional well-being, as well as on the emotional state of others encountered in the course of each mission. As such, counselor Deanna Troi is one of the most important members of Picard's senior staff. Troi's mother is Betazoid diplomat Lwaxana Troi, and her father, Ian Andrew Troi, was a human member of Starfleet. Being of half-Betazoid heritage, Deanna Troi often finds her Betazoid empathic powers to be a source of valuable insight in her job.

MAIN BRIDGE, PART I:
Command and control

The primary control center for the *Starship Enterprise*-D is the Main Bridge, located on the top of the ship's Saucer Module. The bridge is the main duty station for the ship's captain and senior staff. It is from here that the ship is piloted and virtually every vehicle function is managed for the safe, successful execution of each mission.

COMMAND MODULE

The heart of the bridge is the command module, from which the captain, executive officer, and counselor can supervise all bridge operations. The command module also provides two additional seating positions, normally reserved for mission specialists or VIP guests.

THE CAPTAIN'S CHAIR

The captain's chair, located near the center of the bridge, provides the commanding officer direct access to the Ops and Conn stations, and is immediately adjacent to the Executive Officer and the ship's Counselor. The captain's chair armrests include controls for log entries, LCARS operations, viewer control, backup Conn and Ops control, plus armaments and shields.

CAPTAIN JEAN-LUC PICARD

The commanding officer of the *Starship Enterprise*-D is Captain Jean-Luc Picard. A native of LaBarre, France, on Earth, Picard dreamed of exploring the cosmos ever since he was a child. Even as a Starfleet cadet, he attracted the notice of Admiral Hansen, who correctly predicted that Picard would be one of the service's rising stars. Picard's brilliant, deeply ethical leadership has been a key factor in the successful completion of many missions.

MAIN BRIDGE, PART II:
The nerve center

Although the primary responsibility of bridge officers is to provide information to the captain and to execute his or her commands, bridge officers are also responsible for managing specific aspects of the ship's operation from the various bridge control consoles.

MAIN VIEWER

Located at the front of the bridge, this screen provides situational awareness to bridge personnel. It also serves as a display for external communcations. The main viewer generally displays an image of space directly ahead of the ship, but can be used for virtually any desired view or for sensor display.

EMERGENCY TURBOLIFT

A special feature of the *Galaxy*-class explorers, the turbolift provides a swift direct connection between the battle bridge and the main bridge. Located on deck 8, the battle bridge provides for a backup of essential command functions in case of saucer separation.

WESLEY CRUSHER

The son of Chief Medical Officer Beverly Crusher, Wesley Crusher served as an acting ensign on the *Enterprise*-D, prior to his admission to Starfleet Academy. Captain Picard was so impressed with Wesley's intellectual brilliance and his fascination with starship operations, that he not only granted Wesley a field appointment as an acting ensign, but he allowed the boy to serve on the bridge at the Flight Controller station.

CONN

The Flight Controller, or Conn, is the officer who actually flies the ship. This enormously complex task is made manageable by the sophisticated flight control software provided by the Conn console. This station not only provides guidance and navigation, but it coordinates engine operation, both at warp speed and impulse. It also plays a major role during combat situations.

OPS

The Operations Manager, or Ops, is one of the most important stations on the bridge. Ops is responsible for coordinating the needs of each department to be sure that adequate resources are available for all mission needs, and to insure that different mission objectives don't conflict with each other.

DEDICATION PLAQUE

This commemorates the ship's commissioning in 2364. It recognizes the tradition of ships named *Enterprise*, that this is the fifth Federation starship to bear the proud name. Also listed are key personnel who contributed to design and construction, as well as the motto, "to boldly go where no one has gone before," a quote from legendary scientist Zefram Cochrane.

RED ALERT ANNUNCIATOR

These wall display units provide summary of the overall ship's status at a glance to bridge personnel. The bars also serve as Yellow Alert and Red Alert annunciators during crisis situations.

ISOLINEAR SUBPROCESSORS

These cabinets contain racks of isolinear optical chips, the computer modules that support bridge operations. Even if the ship's main computer system should fail, these subprocessors can keep the bridge operational

LIEUTENANT COMMANDER DATA

The senior Operations Officer of the *Enterprise*-D is Lieutenant Commander Data. An android created by legendary cyberneticist Noonien Soong, Data's remarkable intellect and his innate curiosity makes him an invaluable member of the crew.

TACTICAL

The Tactical console, located directly behind the command module, is the station from which the ship's defensive and weapons systems are operated. This includes deflector shields, phaser banks, photon torpedo launchers, as well as the various tactical and security sensor systems. Tactical is also responsible for ship's internal security.

WORF

The *Enterprise*-D tactical officer is Lieutenant Commander Worf. He was just a child when his parents were killed in the Khitomer massacre in 2346. Worf was rescued by Sergey Rozhenko, a human Starfleet officer, who adopted the boy and raised him on Earth. Worf is the only Klingon serving in the Federation Starfleet.

20
368
72
008
407
686
102
23

PROPULSION, MAIN ENGINEERING:
The power to go boldly

For many years, interstellar travel was believed impossible because of the incredible distances between even the nearest stars. Then, in 2063, scientist Zefram Cochrane demonstrated a practical space warp propulsion system that reduced travel time to nearby stars from centuries or millennia to a few years, and eventually even days. Cochrane's breakthrough made it possible for humans to become citizens of the Galaxy.

GEORDI LA FORGE

Lieutenant Commander Geordi La Forge is the chief engineering officer of the *Starship Enterprise*. La Forge is blind, but uses a visual prosthetic device called a VISOR that gives him vision that is superior to most humans. La Forge's technical brilliance and his deep-felt empathy for the men and women under his command make him an unusually effective leader for the ship's engineering department.

DILITHIUM CRYSTALS

Dilithium crystals are used to regulate the matter/antimatter reaction and to create the tuned plasma stream that energizes the subspace field coils in the warp nacelles. In the *Enterprise* warp core, the crystals are mounted in the dilithium crystal articulation frame, a precision device in the matter/antimatter reaction chamber. For many years, dilithium was one of the most valuable substances in the Galaxy because of rarity and because of its role in enabling interstellar travel. Dilithium can now be created by synthetic means, using gamma radiation bombardment, making it much more widely available, and making starflight much more practical.

WARP CORE

The power source for the *Enterprise*-D's warp drive is an advanced matter/antimatter reactor core, which is located in the ship's engineering hull. Reaching some 12 decks in overall height, the core is a chamber in which matter in the form of a hydrogen isotope mixes with its antimatter counterpart. The resulting mutual annihilation creates a tremendous amount of power, as mass is converted into energy as predicted by Einstein's equation, $E=mc^2$.

This energy release occurs in the matter/antimatter reaction chamber, located in the center of the core on Deck 36. At the top of the chamber on Deck 30 is located injectors for matter, while the antimatter injectors are located at the bottom of the chamber, on Deck 42.

In an extreme emergency, the entire core can be ejected from the ship, through a hatch in the bottom of engineering hull.

MASTER SYSTEMS DISPLAY

The master systems display provides a status display, communal work console, and systems terminal for engineering personnel. This station is often used for diagnostics and maintenance, as well as troubleshooting during crisis situations.

CHIEF ENGINEER'S OFFICE

Located immediately adjacent to the warp core, the chief engineer's office provides direct control of the warp drive systems, as well as sophisticated diagnostic and troubleshooting panels. Its central, open design allows close supervision of all engine room personnel.

MASTER SITUATION MONITOR

The master situation monitor displays the status of most of the ship's main systems at a glance. Prominently located in Main Engineering, this large panel provides situational awareness for all engineering personnel.

GALAXY CLASS   U.S.S. ENTERPRISE

NCC-1801-D

WARP FIELD COILS

The subspace "bubble" in which the ship travels while at warp is generated by two sets of powerful field coils, located in the warp nacelles. Each coil is a matched pair of U-shaped verterium cortenide conductors. When injected with pulses of energetic plasma, these coils create a powerful subspace distortion field. By regulating the amount of plasma and the timing of the pulses going to each coil pair, the shape of the subspace field can be controlled, thereby determining speed and direction at faster-than-light speeds.

IMPULSE ENGINE

When the *Enterprise* travels within the confines of a solar system, slower-than-light impulse propulsion is used. Impulse drive uses nuclear fusion, combining hydrogen atoms into helium, which causes the release of tremendous amounts of energy. This is used to expel hydrogen plasma, creating thrust in the same manner as a conventional rocket engine. The impulse engines' fusion reactors also serve as an auxiliary power source for ship's systems.

WARP NACELLES

The two outboard engine pods are known as warp nacelles. They are located away from the main crew module, partly for safety reasons, but also because their position, relative to the rest of the ship, helps to create the subspace field geometry that propels the ship. Inside each nacelle is a row of powerful warp coils, and at the forward tip is a Bussard collector, which harvests interstellar hydrogen as a secondary fuel source.

TACTICAL SYSTEMS:
Influence and control

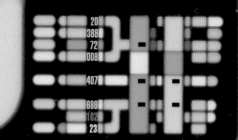

In the hands of a competent Starfleet captain, almost any shipboard system can be turned to some form of tactical advantage now and again. The *Enterprise*-D has a broad array of equipment and weapons systems that are able exert influence on other ships near her in space. Primary weapons are phaser banks, backed up by photon torpedoes. Tractor beams, transporters and separated flight mode provide a range of subtler options. Deflector shields offer main-line defense.

TRACTOR BEAM

Although the tractor beam is normally employed for towing, cargo loading, or proximity maneuvering, it can also have tactical uses, especially for nearby objects.

SEPARATED FLIGHT MODE

In combat situations, the *Enterprise* can separate into two independent spacecraft. The Battle Section, also known as the Stardrive Section, can go into hazardous situations, while the Saucer Module, containing most of the crew and the civilians, can remain behind in relative safety. The Battle Section, commanded from the Battle Bridge, contains the ship's warp drive, both photon torpedo launchers, deflector shields, the main impulse engine, and a full complement of phaser banks. The Saucer Module, which is controlled from the Main Bridge, is propelled by the saucer impulse engines, and also has a full complement of phaser banks and deflectors.

PHOTON TORPEDOES

Photon torpedoes are small missiles containing a matter-antimatter warhead. They employ a small warp sustainer propulsion system, and thus are suitable for use at relativistic and warp speeds. Because of their precision guidance system and adjustable explosive yield, photon torpedoes are extremely flexible weapons, useful in a wide range of tactical situations. The *Enterprise* is equipped with two photon torpedo launchers, one facing forward and the other facing aft. Both are located on the ship's engineering hull.

DEFLECTOR SHIELDS

The ship's primary defense is its powerful deflector shield, which protects the ship against energy and mass based weapons. Unlike the directional navigational deflector, the defensive screens are effective in all directions around the ship.

The energy-based deflectors are powered by direct feeds from both the warp drive system and the impulse engines. Should either power system fail or be unavailable, the other can maintain protection for the ship.

Shields are normally tuned to make them transparent to visible light and sensor beams, but transporter beams cannot pass through them. Deflectors must therefore be deactivated to beam to or from the ship.

PHASER BANKS

Although Starfleet's mission is primarily one of peaceful exploration, voyages into the unknown depths of space sometimes involve encounters with hostile entities. Additionally, the ships of the Starfleet are often called upon to protect Federation interests and citizens. Because of this, the *Enterprise* is equipped with advanced tactical systems.

The ship's primary armament is a complement of phaser banks. These directed energy weapons employ phased energy rectification to create coherent particle beams using the rapid nadion effect.

ROMULAN WARBIRD

One of the fiercest adversary spacecraft confronting the Federation Starfleet, the *D'deridex*-class warbird is the front line vessel of the Romulan Star Empire. Unlike Federation vessels, the Romulan warbird harnesses the Hawking radiation emitted by a quantum singularity, also known as a micro black hole. Although Romulan ships rarely enter Federation territory due to the Neutral Zone treaty, Starfleet captains are always wary of such encounters because of the great power of these ships. Romulan ships are normally equipped with cloaking devices, making them nearly invisible when cloaked.

FERENGI MARAUDER

Although the Ferengi Alliance is not officially regarded as hostile to the Federation, opportunistic commanders of individual Ferengi ships are often known to act against Federation interests. Ferengi *D'Kora*-class marauders, first encountered in 2364 by the *Enterprise*-D near Gamma Tauri IV are powerful vessels, approximately equal in technology to Federation ships. Ferengi ship commanders generally carry the rank of DaiMon.

8819
5325
3096
5604

PERSONAL PHASERS

Personal phasers are Starfleet's standard-issue sidearms. They are energy weapons that can be tuned for a variety of applications. In most security and tactical situations, phasers are set for neural impact, a setting known as "stun," which instantly – but temporarily – renders most humanoids unconscious. Phasers have a number of higher settings, from "heat" to "cut" to "vaporize." The Type-2 phaser is used for most assignments when Starfleet personnel are required to be visibly armed. The smaller, Type-1 phaser can be used when inconspicuous armament is desired, as when on diplomatic missions. Conversely, the Type-3 phaser rifle (left) is available when greater power and range is required.

TRANSPORTER EFFECT

The phase transition of matter into energy involves the controlled release of a tremendous amount of energy. The transporter uses sophisticated molecular imaging scanners to capture the pattern of matter as it dematerializes. This information is used to reassemble the transport subject at its destination. Because of the inherent uncertainty of the position and energy states of any subatomic particle, the Heisenberg compensator must be used to ensure accurate reassembly of atomic patterns.

TRANSPORTER ENHANCER RODS

Because of the extreme precision necessary for successful transport, beaming into areas of electromagnetic interference, or areas occluded by dense matter (such as rock strata) in the beam path can be hazardous. In such cases, transporter operation can be made safer through the use of transporter enhancer rods. These transponder devices are placed in close proximity around the transport subject, providing a more accurate lock for the transporter's targeting scanners.

TRANSPORTER TEST ARTICLE

After systems maintenance, and prior to using a transporter for living beings or valuable cargo, a test article is often employed to verify operation and calibration. Transporter test articles are about a meter in height and are made of pure duranium alloy.

SEQUENCE SELECT

CARGO TRANSPORTER

Eight cargo transporters are located in cargo bays on Decks 4 and on Decks 38 and 39. These units are capable of transporting heavier and larger payloads than personnel transporters, but they do so at a lower imaging resolution, and thus are not suitable for use with living beings. This is known as "molecular resolution," which is adequate for most non-living cargo. When necessary, the cargo transporters can be set to operate at "quantum resolution," to preserve all of the particle states necessary for the accurate transport of living beings.

TRANSPORTER ROOM:
Getting from here to there

For much of the early history of space travel, the relatively short leap from a planet's surface into orbital space was an enormous one. For travelers aboard the *Enterprise* and other Federation ships, this giant leap has been made much faster, easier, and safer by the transporter.

The transporter converts matter into energy, beams that energy into another location, then reassembles the matter into its original form.

TRANSPORTER SYSTEMS SCHEMATIC

The *Galaxy*-class systems schematic tool allows the operator to access detailed output from parametric and magneton scanners as well as the synchronic meter. In addition, it provides detailed information about the state of certain key systems, such as the phase discriminator, biofilter and compensator circuits.

407

686
102
23

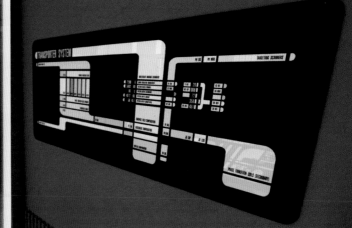

TRANSPORTER CONTROL CONSOLE

The transporter system is controlled from the system operations panel. This station coordinates transporter targeting and manages the dematerialization and rematerialization cycles. It also monitors the function of pattern buffers and other subsystems. Although the transporter system is highly automated, a trained operator is required because of the ever-present possibility of malfunction.

SHUTTLECRAFT AND SHUTTLEBAYS:
Versatile short-range transport

8819210
5325406
3096700

The *U.S.S. Enterprise* is equipped with three shuttlebays and a full complement of short-range shuttle vehicles. Although the transporter is used for most short-range conveyance to and from the ship, there are times when an auxiliary vehicle is preferred.

The main shuttlebay is located on deck 4 of the Saucer Module. This massive facility is the base of operation for most of the ship's complement of shuttlecraft and shuttlepods. Two smaller secondary shuttlebays are located on Deck 13 of the Stardrive Section. Starfleet shuttles are traditionally named for explorers, scientists, and artists.

TYPE 6 PERSONNEL SHUTTLECRAFT

Although older in design than the Type 7, many shuttle pilots prefer the Type 6 because of its airbreathing thrusters that significantly improve performance in atmospheric flight. In a suitable atmosphere, ambient air is ingested by the forward inputs. High-energy plasma from the engine core heats and compresses the air, which is then exhausted as reaction mass through the aft vents.

TYPE 7 PERSONNEL SHUTTLECRAFT

The Type 7 shuttlecraft is the most modern version of the personnel shuttle carried aboard the *Enterprise*. With a flight crew of two and capable of carrying up to six passengers, the Type 7 shuttle is normally capable of low warp speeds across ranges of approximately 20 light-days.

TYPE 15 SHUTTLEPOD

Even though they are the smallest of the personnel shuttles, most pilots will tell you that the Type 15 shuttlepods are surprisingly sporty and fun to fly. Boasting a thrust-to-mass ratio 50% greater than the Type 6 shuttles, the Type 15 shuttlepod is a high-performance, if short range vehicle.

SHUTTLE LAUNCH

An airtight structural hatch normally seals the shuttlebay, protecting the bay's interior and keeping air inside. However, when the bay is actually supporting flight operations the big door is opened to space, and a forcefield is used to keep air inside the bay.

TRACTOR BEAM

The delicate job of piloting the first few meters of a shuttle's flight or the last few meters before landing is critical, indeed. Because even a minor pilot error could cause major damage to the *Enterprise*, launch and final approach is accomplished under computer control, using precision tractor beam emitters.

OTHER SHUTTLEBAY OPERATIONS

In addition to supporting shuttle flight operations and maintenance, the *Enterprise* shuttlebays can also be used for a wide variety of other functions. For example, an instrumented probe, designed by noted scientist Paul Stubbs to study surface eruptions on a red giant star, was prepped and launched from one of the *Enterprise* shuttlebays.

SHUTTLE LANDING

Most shuttle vehicles are capable of independent entry and liftoff from the surface of a Class M (Earth-like) planet. The shuttle's main propulsion system is usually throttled down to nearly zero during final approach. Low-yield antigrav generators and tractor emitters are used to lower the shuttle gently to touchdown, and then again for liftoff. This protects the landing site and any bystanders from damage or injury from impulse thrusters.

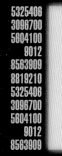

5325406
3096700
5604100
9012
8563909
8819210
5325406
3096700
5604100
9012
8563909

SHUTTLEBAYS 2 AND 3

Two secondary shuttlebays are located on Deck 13 of the ship's Stardrive Section. These smaller bays provide redundancy to the Main Shuttlebay, and also provide support for auxiliary vehicles for the Stardrive Section during separated flight mode.

20
368

SHUTTLE COCKPIT

Shuttle avionics and control systems are based on a subset of the LCARS operating system that is used throughout the *Enterprise*. Although the flight computers are capable of autonomous operation, Starfleet flight rules general require a pilot and usually a copilot on most missions.

	1728191
	8819210
340	5325406
6	3096700
640	5604100
712	9012
781	8563909
102	1072820
88	0177

MEDICAL DEPARTMENT

More properly called the Medical Department, the *Enterprise* sickbay facilities are located on Deck 12 of the Saucer Module. Sickbay provides the full spectrum of medical care from routine examination to intensive care. Under the supervision of Chief Medical Officer Beverly Crusher, sickbay also includes an advanced biomedical research laboratory.

MASTER MONITOR

Providing convenient access to detailed information about all patients in ICU, this is a hub for any material that the doctor in charge requires. Although each bed has its own informatics, the Master Monitor provides a way to access overview data, trends, and deeper layers of material as necessary.

DR. BEVERLY CRUSHER

Dr. Beverly Crusher is the Chief Medical Officer of the *Starship Enterprise*-D. The onetime head of Starfleet Medical, Crusher was born in Copernicus City, Luna and graduated at the top of her class at Starfleet's medical school. Crusher was raised at the Arvada III colony, where she credits her grandmother with teaching her the value of nontraditional medicine, including the use of herbs and roots.

SURGICAL AND EXAM TABLE

Sickbay's intensive care ward features a multipurpose surgical and examination table, designed to facilitate routine diagnosis as well as a wide range of surgical procedures. Located directly above the adjustable table is a ceiling-mounted cluster of sensor, imaging, and forcefield devices available to the physician.

SICKBAY
Healing and helping the crew

Space exploration is an inherently dangerous enterprise. Missions into the unknown inevitably expose explorers to unexpected hazards. Space travel and shipboard life has its own risks, and even routine health care for a crew, attached personnel, and passengers is of vital importance. Meeting these challenges is an essential part of the ship's mission and is the responsibility of those who work in the ship's Sickbay.

DIAGNOSTIC BIO-BEDS
Patient beds in the intensive care ward incorporate sophisticated sensor devices to provide realtime monitoring and display of biomedical data. They also provide access to utilities such as oxygen, specialized breathing mixtures, isolation fields, intravenous fluids, forcebeam traction therapy, and local gravity control.

DOCTOR'S OFFICE
Contrasting with the frequently urgent atmosphere of Sickbay and the Medical Lab, the Chief Medical Officer's office provides a quiet place for work and for private consultations.

20
368
72
008

SCIENCE LABORATORIES:
Centers for discovery

The mission of the *Enterprise* – to explore the unknown – often involves detailed scientific analysis. For this reason, the ship is equipped with a wide range of scientific laboratories, spanning the spectrum from biology and geology, to engineering and even quantum mechanics, all staffed by specialists in their fields.

A good example of success was when Medical Laboratory personnel, under the direction of Dr. Beverly Crusher (with Engineering specialists) were responsible for the safe recovery of Captain Jean-Luc Picard after he had been assimilated into the Borg Collective. Precision microsurgical techniques and molecular engineering processes were employed to remove the microcircuit fibers and nanoprobe devices. This was the first known instance of a Borg drone being successfully disengaged from the Collective without causing the death of the patient.

8819210
5325406
3096700
5604100
9012
8563909
5325406
3096700
5604100
9012
8563909
8819210
5325406
3096700
5604100
9012
8563909

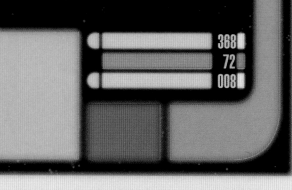

SHORT-RANGE SENSOR ARRAY

Located all around the primary and secondary hulls, the short-range sensor array is a collection of modular pallets containing a wide range of scientific and tactical sensor instruments. These instruments are easily upgradeable when new technologies become available, or when needed for specific mission requirements.

TRICORDER

One of the must useful tools for starship personnel, the tricorder combines handheld sensors with portable recorder and computer devices. Field tricorders are invaluable for scientific and tactical analysis on away missions to planetary surfaces, while specialized medical and engineering tricorders are essential tools for many shipboard crew members.

LONG-RANGE SENSOR

Located at the front of the Engineering Hull, the long-range sensor is built into the massive reflector of the navigational deflector. The long-range sensor's primary job is to look ahead in the ship's flight path to detect potential hazards such as meteroids or debris, as well as to gather information about the ship's destination.

SPECTRAL ANALYSIS TOOL

Geologists often make use of the spectral analysis tool to vaporize small rock samples. The resulting light emissions can yield detailed information about the rock's composition, and the vapor residue can be analyzed to provide information about molecular traces.

GEOLOGY LAB

The Planetary Geosciences lab specializes in the study of terrestrial planet structures and the processes that form them. The laboratory includes equipment to analyze rock specimens, as well sensor systems to map and to study the large-scale structures of planetary bodies.

MEDICAL LAB

The Medical Laboratory supports crew health care, specific mission objectives, and general scientific research. The main laboratory is located adjacent to sickbay on Deck 12, with additional facilities located throughout the ship. In crisis situations, the Biomedical Laboratory is often a key player in protecting the crew from the danger of unknown alien pathogens or environmental hazards. In extreme cases, the Medical Lab can literally be the difference between life and death for the crew. The Medical Laboratory plays an important role in life-form characterization and analysis, which is a key part of the *Enterprise*'s mission of exploration. Laboratory personnel are often called upon to help diagnose diseases afflicting newly-discovered life-forms, meaning that they need to characterize not only the new form, but the disease mechanism as well, before it is possible to devise treatment.

ENGINEERING LAB

Engineering labs provide research and testing equipment needed to develop and maintain field-customized equipment, as well as to analyze technology from newly-encountered alien cultures.

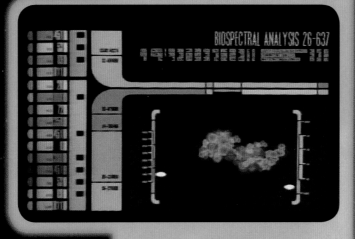

ABOVE: THE SPECTRAL ANALYSIS TOOL, CAUGHT IN THE ACT OF SCANNING A GEOLOGICAL SAMPLE FOR CRITICAL DATA.

LIVING QUARTERS:
A touch of home

Starship duty can be long, difficult, and hazardous. Even "routine" missions require all personnel to be at top readiness for extended periods, for the hazards of space exploration can be sudden, indeed. That's why Starfleet takes such care to provide comfortable living quarters for its people.

Each crew member is encouraged to decorate his or her quarters with individual touches reflecting his or her personality and tastes. Many crew choose décor that hints of their home or their family.

Although the captain's quarters is the largest on the ship, each crew member has living accommodations that astronauts on earlier starships might have considered to be luxurious. Captain Picard's suite on Deck 6 comprises five rooms, including an office, and is located at the front of the saucer section, with windows that provide a dramatic vista of space ahead.

JEAN-LUC PICARD

Picard's love of literature can be seen in his collection of ancient paper books, as well as a small decorative bust of Earth writer and poet, William Shakespeare. His interest in ancient mariners is reflected by his possession of an ancient sextant, a navigational device used by early ocean-going explorers. Perhaps the most unusual bit of décor in Picard's quarters is a small decorative tapestry presented to him by the natives of planet Mintaka III. Senior officers and VIP passengers are usually also assigned to suites on Deck 6.

JUNIOR OFFICERS' QUARTERS

Junior officers and other crew personnel are usually assigned to smaller – but still very comfortable – living quarters throughout the ship. Although most crew accommodations are located in the Primary (Saucer) Hull, the Stardrive Section includes sufficient quarters for personnel required during separated flight mode.

WILLIAM RIKER

Commander Riker's love of life is exemplified by his trombone, a musical instrument popular on Earth.

DATA

Data's quest to understand humanity has led him to undertake such diverse hobbies as painting and holodeck roleplaying of characters from Sir Arthur Conan Doyle's Sherlock Holmes stories.

U.S.S. ENTERPRISE

GALAXY-CLASS NCC-1701-D

A fore and aft view of the *U.S.S. Enterprise* NCC-1701-D. The warp drive nacelles provide the core motive thrust for the ship, but all that power would be totally wasted without the long-range sensor which dominates the base of the ship. It's a big universe, but it would be lethally dangerous to go charging off blindly at warp speed if you weren't very sure indeed of where you were going. The impulse engines, more traditional in their operation, face aft, above the main engineering hull.

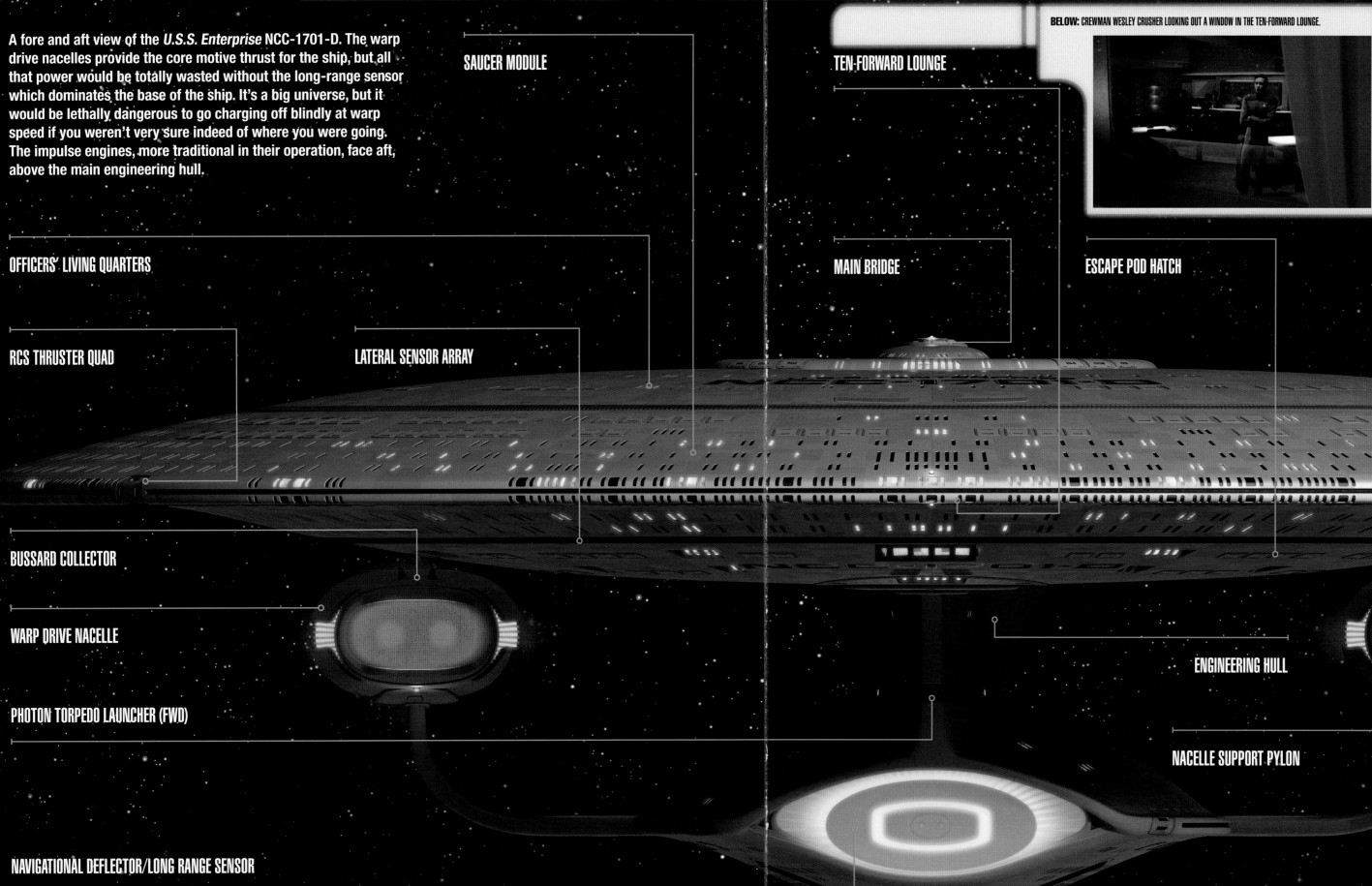

BELOW: CREWMAN WESLEY CRUSHER LOOKING OUT A WINDOW IN THE TEN-FORWARD LOUNGE.

SAUCER MODULE

TEN-FORWARD LOUNGE

OFFICERS' LIVING QUARTERS

MAIN BRIDGE

ESCAPE POD HATCH

PHASER BANK

RCS THRUSTER QUAD

LATERAL SENSOR ARRAY

BUSSARD COLLECTOR

WARP DRIVE NACELLE

ENGINEERING HULL

PHOTON TORPEDO LAUNCHER (FWD)

NACELLE SUPPORT PYLON

NAVIGATIONAL DEFLECTOR/LONG RANGE SENSOR

TEN-FORWARD:
Off-duty view of the cosmos

Located on the front edge of the ship's Saucer Module on Deck 10, the Ten-Forward Lounge is the social center for the *Enterprise* crew during off-duty hours. Whether a quiet setting for a relaxing after-work drink, a casual meeting place for a snack with friends, or listening to a musical entertainment performed by fellow crew members, Ten-Forward is the place to be.

Ten-Forward features large windows that frame a dramatic view of the cosmos, and thus is also a perfect place for quiet meditation and contemplation.

WORF
Worf, a native of the Klingon Empire, takes pride in his heritage through his display of the traditional bat'leth sword. According to legend, Kahless the Unforgettable plunged a lock of his hair into a river of lava from the Kri'stak volcano, then quenched it in the Lake of Lursa, twisting it to form a blade.

REPLICATOR
Food service in living quarters is provided by a replicator terminal. Not only does the replicator provide an extremely wide range of food and beverage choices, but the use of replicator technology results in a significant savings of weight and space in the ship for food storage, as well as for the equipment and personnel that would otherwise be required for food preparation and delivery.

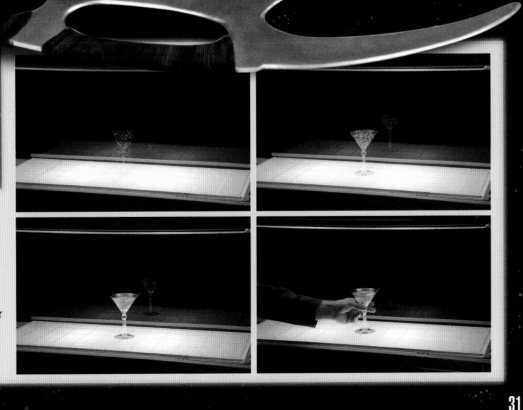

WEDDING
The wedding of transporter chief Miles O'Brien and botanist Keiko Ishikawa was held in Ten-Forward. Reflecting the heritage of the bride and the groom, their wedding ceremony combined traditions from Earth's Irish and Japanese cultures.

REPLICATOR
Replicator terminals provide nearly every imaginable form of food and drink. Ten-Forward's replicator matrices include a delightfully broad range of exotic food and beverages, from Aldeberan whiskey to a Mareuvian tea, and even prune juice. Even traditional Klingon cuisine can be replicated with near-perfect fidelity and taste. Be sure to try the Thalian chocolate mousse.

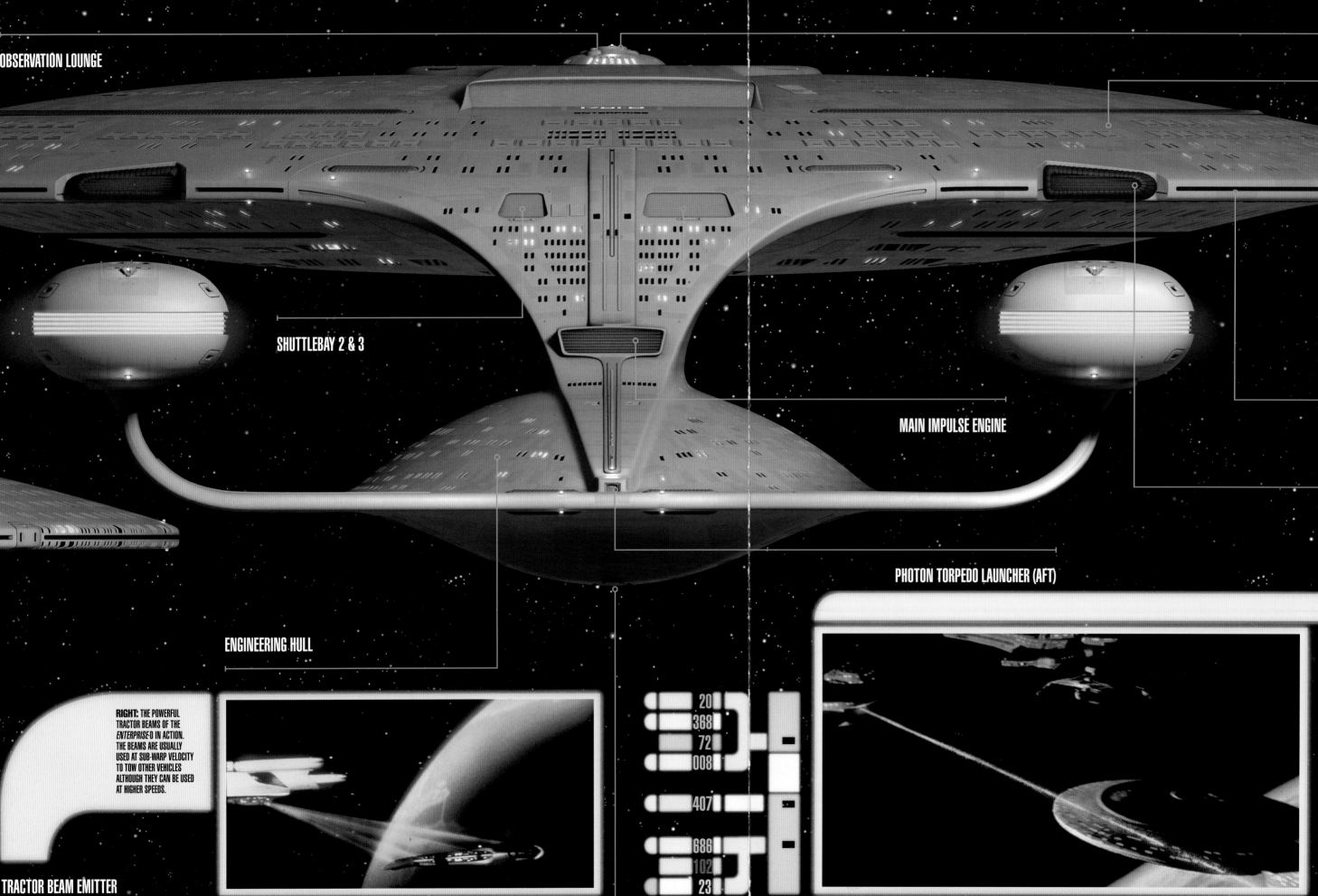

OBSERVATION LOUNGE

MAIN BRIDGE

SAUCER MODULE

SHUTTLEBAY 2 & 3

MAIN IMPULSE ENGINE

PHASER BANK

SAUCER IMPULSE ENGINE

PHOTON TORPEDO LAUNCHER (AFT)

ENGINEERING HULL

RIGHT: THE POWERFUL TRACTOR BEAMS OF THE *ENTERPRISE*-D IN ACTION. THE BEAMS ARE USUALLY USED AT SUB-WARP VELOCITY TO TOW OTHER VEHICLES ALTHOUGH THEY CAN BE USED AT HIGHER SPEEDS.

TRACTOR BEAM EMITTER

LEFT: THE *ENTERPRISE*-D HAS COME UNDER ATTACK ON A NUMBER OF OCCASIONS. THIS IMAGE, CAUGHT DURING BATTLE, SHOWS A PHASER BEAM PASSING OVER THE BOW.

20
368
72
008

407

686
102
23

SYNTHEHOL

Although traditional alcoholic beverages are available at Ten-Forward, most crew members prefer synthehol-based drink. Synthehol, invented by the Ferengi, provides mild intoxication in humanoids, similar to alcohol, but without the deleterious effects.

5325406
3096700
5604100
9012
8563909
8819210
5325406
3096700
5604100
9012
8563909

3D CHESS

A favorite form of relaxation in Ten-Forward is the traditional game of three-dimensional chess. Like its two-dimensional ancestor, it is a game of strategy and wills, based on symbols from medieval Earth warfare.

340
6
640
712
781

GUINAN

The hostess of the Ten-Forward lounge, Guinan is a civilian of El-Aurian descent. Like many good bartenders, she is a quiet, insightful personality, which has helped her to become friends with many crew members. Indeed, Guinan has been one of Captain Picard's most trusted advisors for many years.

210
406
700
100
012
909

MUSIC

Ten-Forward also provides a musical venue for the creative energies of crew members of the ship's crew, which in turn makes for a pleasant evening's entertainment. Be it a classical Earth quartet or graceful Algolian ceremonial rhythms.

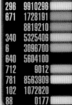

001   0019210
296   9910296
671   1728191
       8819210
340   5325406
6   3096700
640   5604100
712   9012
781   8563909
102   1072820
88   0177

HOLODECK:
Virtual reality recreation & training

```
                    1728191
                    8819210
              340   5325406
              6     3096700
              640   5604100
              712      9012
              781   8563909
              102   1072820
              88       0177
```

Off-duty crew members on the *U.S.S. Enterprise* often choose to spend time on the holodeck. Also known as the holographic environment simulator, the holodeck provides near-perfect re-creations of nearly any setting, as well as amazingly realistic interactive replicas of people. There are literally thousands of environments stored in computer memory, any one of which can be presented in the holodeck with startling realism.

The biggest advance in the *Enterprise* holodecks over previous simulators is sophisticated artificial intelligence software. This means that holodecks can now include startlingly realistic human characters. Unlike simple images, these characters can interact with holodeck participants, taking on roles as exercise partners, characters from fictional stories, even new characters from the participant's own imagination.

HOLODECK GRID
The holodeck uses three-dimensional projection to create near-perfect images of settings from ancient forests to modern starships. Holographic forcebeam imagery is used to give the illusion of physical solidity to objects, so you can't walk through walls. (Unless, of course, walking through walls is part of the simulation!)

Many simulations are designed so that objects in the distance appear much further away than the holodeck walls. Often, these simulations use a "treadmill" effect, allowing participants to traverse great distances, while remaining in the center of the relatively small holodeck.

AIKIDO TRAINING
A holographic sparring partner provides training and exercise in the traditional Japanese martial art, adjustable to the participant's skill level.

ENTERPRISE BRIDGE
Historically-accurate simulation of the bridge the most famous starship in Federation history, the original NCC-1701 as she was with Captain James Kirk at the helm.

```
              001   0019210
              296   9910296
              671   1728191
                    8819210
              340   5325406
              6     3096700
              640   5604100
              712      9012
              781   8563909
```

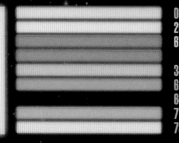

The holodeck provides virtually limitless simulated environments, including:

KLINGON AGE OF ASCENSION
The ancient ritual in which a Klingon warrior comes of age and takes his or her place as a full member of Klingon society.

SAILING SHIP *ENTERPRISE*
One of the first ships to bear the name *Enterprise*, an 18th century oceangoing merchant sloop.

ALPINE SKIING
Experienced on a startlingly realistic simulation of a famous mountain range on Earth's European continent.

CAFÉ DES ARTISTES
Contemporary outdoor restaurant located in the city of Paris on Earth, in the shadow of the Eiffel Tower. Try the Croissants d'ilithium!

SHERLOCK HOLMES
Enter the 19th century world of Sherlock Holmes, England's greatest consulting detective, from the literary works of Sir Arthur Conan Doyle.

DIXON HILL
The hard-boiled world of fictional detective Dixon Hill, solving mysteries in Earth's 20th century city of San Francisco.

POKER WITH GREAT SCIENTISTS
The classic Earth game of chance and of human will, as experienced with historically-accurate simulations of four of Earth's great scientists, Isaac Newton, Albert Einstein, and Stephen Hawking.

ROUSSEAU ASTEROID BELT
A magnificent asteroid field near planet Rousseau V, located in the midst of a neutrino cloud. Be sure to see the spectacular harmonic resonance, when the sky actually seems to sing!

VIRUS CONTAINMENT MODULE

This unusual piece of cargo was carried aboard the *Enterprise*. The actual cargo was a collection of highly dangerous disease viruses. The *Enterprise* transported the viruses, in this containment module, to the Rachelis system for vital medical research.

CARGO HANDLING

A handy antigrav pallet can be used for handling of small cargo modules and other pieces of equipment. Similar pallets are used by sickbay personnel for medical transport of patients.

CARGO MODULES

Most cargo is shipped in a variety of standardized containers designed for easy handling and to protect the cargo from damage and contamination, and to prevent the cargo from damaging or contaminating other cargo modules.

CARGO TRANSPORTER

Most cargo is loaded and offloaded by means of a cargo transporter. To save energy, cargo transporters are normally set to use "molecular resolution" beaming, instead of the quantum resolution that is used when transporting life forms. However, cargo transporters can be set for quantum resolution when needed.

CARGO BAY:
Delivering the goods

The *Enterprise* is a multi-mission ship, and in fact often conducts several missions simultaneously. This is why the ship is equipped for such a wide range of functions. One of the *Enterprise*'s most important functions is one of its least glamorous, that of carrying cargo to distant destinations. Although it's usually more efficient to use a dedicated cargo ship for bulk material, the speed and flexibility of a starship makes it ideal in critical situations to deliver vitally-needed supplies.

COLONISTS
The cargo bays are among the largest open spaces on board the *Enterprise*. When needed, they can be used to house large numbers of passengers or colonists for short trips or until regular guest quarters can be prepared.

SHIP'S SERVICES
Corridors, turbolifts, and more

20	720	0203451
00	891	0019281
00	451	0019281

Starship interior planning is an art as much as it is a science. Maximizing the useful space available is as complex as it is critical. Typically, radial corridors run from the center of a deck towards the hull, and concentric corridors lie in hull-shaped loops of increasing size. Radial corridors provide access to supply lines and cabling ducts, whilst concentric ones contain personnel support.

CORRIDORS

Ship's services and infrastructure includes many different systems that support the crew and the ship's primary operation. One such infrastructure system is the ship's corridors. You might think of the corridors as just being empty space, but in fact, they are a surprisingly complex system. Connecting the entire habitable volume of the ship, corridors provide life support, temperature control, illumination, and artificial gravity. They also have data connectivity, security sensor systems, as well as fire control and security isolation forcefields. Corridor wall panels can be opened to provide access to utilities and other systems for maintenance.

JEFFERIES TUBE

Although most of the ship's systems are designed to provide easy access for maintenance and repair, there are portions of the ship that are relatively inaccessible. For such areas, service crawlways, also known as Jefferies tubes, are provided.

TURBOLIFT

The *Enterprise* is a big ship. The turbolift system helps crew members get where they need to be, when they need to be there. Turbolifts provide high speed transport to all decks, and along the length of the entire ship.

STRUCTURAL INTEGRITY FIELD AND INERTIAL DAMPERS

The acceleration created by the ship's propulsion systems is so powerful that even the impulse drive would instantly tear the ship apart and pulverize the crew. To keep the ship together and protect the crew, force field generators create a structural integrity field and an inertial damper field. The first greatly strengthens the ship's skeleton and skin, while the second absorbs most of the forces created when the ship changes speed or direction.

REPLICATOR TERMINAL

The ship's replicator system provides food, beverages, supplies, tools, and spare parts by converting energy into matter, using pre-stored patterns, very much like the ship's transporter. This is far more efficient than carrying all of the materials necessary to support the crew and operations for an extended mission in deep space. The replicator gives the crew an extremely wide range of both culinary choices, as well as supplies and parts, limited only by the computer's database.

LIFE SUPPORT

Perhaps the least glamorous, yet most important system on the ship is life support. More properly known as environmental systems, life support includes the systems that maintain and recycle the ship's breathable atmosphere, temperature control systems, and water purification and recycling. As you might expect, the ship has several independent life support systems, so that if one fails, others can keep the crew alive.

ARTIFICIAL GRAVITY

Although a zero-gravity environment can be fun, long-term exposure to microgravity can be harmful to life-forms that have evolved on a planetary surface. That's why artificial gravity generators provide a stable gravitational environment for the crew throughout the ship.

ISOLINEAR OPTICAL CHIP

Isolinear optical chips are compact information storage and processing devices. These devices are made from linear memory crystal, using holographic optical storage technology, and are capable of storing and processing 2.15 kiloquads of data. Isolinear chips are found throughout the ship's computer systems, and are also used for handy portable information storage.

PERSONAL COMMUNICATOR

An integral part of every crew member's Starfleet uniform, the personal communicator badge provides not only voice contact, but also serves as a locator for security and transporter systems. The communicator can be activated by touch or by voice command.

451

INTO THE NEXT GENERATION
Who knows what tomorrow will bring?

Why explore space? The need to discover what lies over the next hill is fundamental to humans and to nearly every intelligent species known. The *Starship Enterprise* and her sister ships are perhaps the greatest expressions of this passion for knowledge. And in making their voyages of discovery, we have found a nearly endless stream of benefits for all. Our society enjoys new resources, new technologies, new philosophies, new friendships, and much more, all because of our ongoing need to expand our horizons. No wonder space exploration attracts the best and the brightest of our people, and why it requires the most advanced of our starships.

The *Enterprise* is one of the most extraordinary ships ever created for exploration, but it is only the latest in a long line of extraordinary ships.

Who knows that, even more extraordinary ships will help us delve even further into the unknown? And who knows what amazing wonders we will find on the final frontier?

THE STORY OF
Little
Red Riding
Hood

THE BROTHERS GRIMM
ILLUSTRATED BY
CHRISTOPHER BING

HANDPRINT  BOOKS

AN IMPRINT OF
CHRONICLE BOOKS • SAN FRANCISCO

ONCE UPON A TIME there was a charming little girl. Everyone who set eyes on her adored her. The person who loved her most of all was her grandmother, and she was always giving her presents. Once she made her a little hood of red velvet. It was so becoming that the girl wanted to wear it all the time, and so she came to be called Little Red Riding Hood.

One day, the girl's mother said to her, "Little Red Riding Hood, here are some cakes and a bottle of wine. Take them to your grandmother. She's ill and feels

Ex Libris

Library of Congress Cataloging-in-Publication Data
Bing, Christopher H.
The story of Little Red Riding Hood / by Christopher Bing.
p.   cm.
Summary: A little girl meets a wolf in the forest on her way to visit her grandmother.
ISBN 978-0-8118-6986-7
[1. Fairy tales. 2. Folklore.] I. Little Red Riding Hood. English. II. Title.
PZ8.B5346St 2010   398.20945'02—dc22   [E]   2009019577

Manufactured by Toppan Leefung,
Da Ling Shan Town, Dongguan, China, in July 2010.

1 3 5 7 9 10 8 6 4 2

This product conforms to CPSIA 2008.

Chronicle Books LLC
680 Second Street, San Francisco, California 94107
www.chroniclekids.com

This book is for Tessa, my inspirational muse for Little Red Riding Hood and one-third of my wife Wendy's and my heart's song to the future of mankind.

weak, and they will make her strong. You'd better start off now, before it gets too hot, and when you're out in the woods, look straight ahead of you like a good little girl and don't stray from the path. Otherwise you'll fall and break the bottle, and then there'll be nothing for Grandmother. And when you walk into her parlor, don't forget to say good morning, and don't go poking around in all the corners of the house."

"I'll do just as you say," Little Red Riding Hood promised her mother.

Grandmother lived deep in the woods, about half an hour's walk from the village. No sooner had Little Red Riding Hood set foot in the forest than she met the wolf. Little Red Riding Hood had no idea what a wicked beast he was, and so she wasn't in the least afraid of him.

"Good morning, Little Red Riding Hood," the wolf said.

"Thank you kindly, Mr. Wolf," she replied.

"Where are you headed so early this morning, Little Red Riding Hood?"

"To Grandmother's house," she replied.

"What's that tucked under your apron?"

"Some cakes and wine. Yesterday we baked, and Grandmother, who is ill and feeling weak, needs something to make her better," she replied.

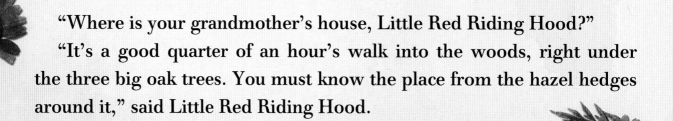

"Where is your grandmother's house, Little Red Riding Hood?"

"It's a good quarter of an hour's walk into the woods, right under the three big oak trees. You must know the place from the hazel hedges around it," said Little Red Riding Hood.

The wolf thought to himself, "That tender young thing will make a nice dainty snack! She'll taste even better than the old woman. If you're really crafty, you'll get them both."

The wolf walked alongside Little Red Riding Hood for a while. Then he said, "Little Red Riding Hood, have you noticed the beautiful flowers all around? Why don't you stay and look at them for a while? I don't

think you've even heard how sweetly the birds are singing. You're acting as if you were on the way to school, when it's so much fun out here in the woods."

Little Red Riding Hood looked with eyes wide open and noticed how the sunbeams were dancing in the trees. She caught sight of the beautiful flowers all around and thought, "If you bring Grandmother a fresh bouquet, she'll be overjoyed. It's still so early in the morning that I'm sure to get there in plenty of time."

Little Red Riding Hood left the path and ran off into the woods looking for flowers. As soon as she had picked one, she caught sight of an even more beautiful one somewhere else and went after it. And so she went ever deeper into the woods.

The wolf ran straight to Grandmother's house and knocked at the door.

"Who's there?"

"Little Red Riding Hood. I've brought some cakes and wine. Open the door."

"Just raise the latch," Grandmother called out. "I'm too weak to get out of bed."

The wolf raised the latch, and the door swung wide open. Without saying a word, he went straight to Grandmother's bed and gobbled her right up. Then he put on her clothes and her nightcap, lay down in her bed, and drew the curtains.

Meanwhile, Little Red Riding Hood was running around looking for flowers. When she had so many in her arms that she couldn't carry any more, she suddenly remembered Grandmother and got back on the path leading to her house. She was surprised to find the door open,

and when she stepped into the house, she had such a strange feeling that she thought, "Oh, my goodness, I'm usually so glad to be at Grandmother's house, but today I feel really uncomfortable."

Little Red Riding Hood called out a hello, but there was no reply.

Then she went over to the bed and pulled back the curtains.
Grandmother was lying there with her nightcap pulled down
over her face. She looked very strange.

"Oh, Grandmother, what big ears you have!"
"The better to hear you with."
"Oh, Grandmother, what big eyes you have!"
"The better to see you with."

"Oh, Grandmother, what big hands you have!"

"The better to grab you with!"

"Oh, Grandmother, what a big scary mouth you have!"

"The better to eat you with!"

No sooner had the wolf said these words than he leaped out of
bed and gobbled up poor Little Red Riding Hood.

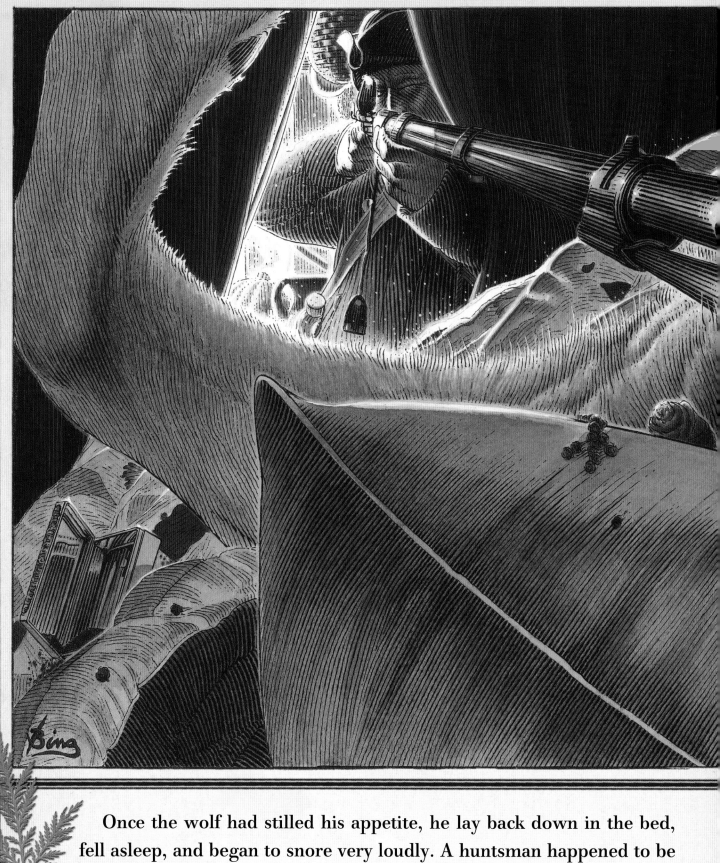

Once the wolf had stilled his appetite, he lay back down in the bed, fell asleep, and began to snore very loudly. A huntsman happened to be passing by the house just then and thought, "How loudly the old woman is snoring! I'd better check to see if anything's wrong." He walked into the house and, when he reached the bed, he realized that a wolf was lying in it.

"I've found you at last, you old sinner," he said. "I've been after you for a long time now."

He pulled out his musket and was about to take aim when he realized that the wolf might have eaten Grandmother and that he could still save her.

Instead of firing, he took out a pair of scissors and began cutting open the belly of the sleeping wolf. After making a few cuts, he caught sight of a red cap. He made a few more cuts, and a girl leaped out, crying, "Oh, I was so terrified! It was so dark in the belly of the wolf."

Although she could barely breathe, the aged grandmother also found her way back out of the belly. Little Red Riding Hood quickly fetched some large stones and filled the wolf's belly with them. When the wolf awoke, he tried to race off, but the stones were so heavy that his legs collapsed, and he fell down dead.

Little Red Riding Hood, her grandmother, and the huntsman were elated. The huntsman skinned the wolf and took the pelt home with him. Grandmother ate the cakes and drank the wine that Little Red Riding

Hood had brought her and recovered her health. Little Red Riding Hood said to herself, "Never again will you stray from the path and go into the woods when your mother has forbidden it."

*T*here is a story about another time that Little Red Riding Hood met a wolf on the way to Grandmother's house, while she was bringing her some cakes. The wolf tried to get her to stray from the path, but Little Red Riding Hood was on her guard and kept right on going. She told her grandmother that she had met a wolf and that he had greeted her. But he had looked at her in such an evil way that, "If we hadn't been out in the open, he would have gobbled me right up."

"Well then," said Grandmother. "We'll just lock the door so he can't get in."

A little while later the wolf knocked at the door and called out, "Open the door, Grandmother. It's Little Red Riding Hood, and I'm bringing you some cakes."

The two kept completely quiet and refused to open the door. Then old Graybeard circled the house a few times and jumped up on the roof. He was planning on waiting until Little Red Riding Hood went home. Then he was going to creep after her and gobble her up in the dark.

But Grandmother figured out what was on his mind.
There was a big stone trough in front of the house.
Grandmother said to the child, "Here's a bucket, Little
Red Riding Hood. Yesterday I cooked some sausages in it.
Take the water in which they were boiled and pour it into
the trough."

Little Red Riding Hood kept taking water to the trough
until it was completely full. The smell from those sausages
reached the wolf's nostrils.

His neck was stretched out so far from sniffing and looking around that he lost his balance and began to slide down the roof. He slid right down into the trough and was drowned. Little Red Riding Hood walked home cheerfully, and no one ever did her any harm.

The Tale of
Little Red Riding Hood

by Charles Perrault

Once upon a time there was a village girl, the prettiest you can imagine. Her mother adored her. Her grandmother adored her even more and made a little red hood for her. The hood suited the child so well that everywhere she went she was known by the name Little Red Riding Hood.

One day her mother baked some cakes and said to her: "I want you to go and see how your grandmother is faring, for I've heard that she's ill. Take her some cakes and this little pot of butter."

Little Red Riding Hood left right away for her grandmother's house, which was in another village. As she was walking through the woods, she met old Neighbor Wolf, who wanted to eat her right there on the spot. But he didn't dare, because some woodcutters were in the forest.

He asked where she was going. The poor child, who did not know that it was dangerous to stop and listen to wolves, said: "I'm going to go see my grandmother. And I'm taking her some cakes and a little pot of butter sent by my mother."

"Does she live very far away?" asked the wolf.